Hume David

The life of David Hume

Hume David

The life of David Hume

ISBN/EAN: 9783741197529

Manufactured in Europe, USA, Canada, Australia, Japa

Cover: Foto ©Raphael Reischuk / pixelio.de

Manufactured and distributed by brebook publishing software
(www.brebook.com)

Hume David

The life of David Hume

Published by the same Author,

The History of England, from the In-
vafion of *Julius Cæfar* to the Revolution :
A new Edition, printed on fine Paper,
with many Corrections and Additions,
and a complete Index, 8 vols. Royal
Paper, 4to. 7l. 7s.

*** Another Edition on fmall Paper,
4to. 4l. 10s.

*** Another Edition, 8 vols. 8vo. 2l. 8s.

Effays and Treatifes on feveral Subjects,
with an Index, 2 vols. Royal Paper.
4to. 1l. 16s.

*** Another Edition, 2 vols. 8vo. 12s.

*** Another Edition, 4 vols. fmall
8vo. 14s.

Printed for T. CADELL in the Strand.

DAVID HUME, Esq.

OF

DAVID HUME, E[SQ.]

WR[ITTEN BY] H[IMSE]LF.

LONDON:

PRINTED FOR W. STRAHAN, AND
T. CADELL, IN THE STRAND.

MDCCLXXVII.

MR. HUME, a few months before his death, wrote the following fhort account of his own Life; and, in a codicil to his will, defired that it might be prefixed to the next edition of his Works. That edition cannot be publifhed for a confiderable time. The Editor, in the mean while, in order to ferve the pur-

chafers

chafers of the former editions ; and, at the fame
time, to gratify the impatience of the public curiofity ;
has thought proper to pub-
lifh it feparately, without al-
tering even the title or fuper-
fcription, which was written
in Mr. Hume's own hand on
the cover of the manufcript.

M Y

MY OWN

LIFE.

IT is difficult for a man to
speak long of himself without vanity; therefore, I shall be
short. It may be thought an in-
stance of vanity that I pretend at
all to write my life; but this
Narrative shall contain little more
than the History of my Writings;

B

as, indeed, almoſt all my life has been ſpent in literary pur-ſuits and occupations. The firſt ſuccefs of moſt of my writings was not ſuch as to be an object of vanity.

I was born the 26th of April 1711, old ſtyle, at Edinburgh. I was of a good family, both by father and mother: my father's family is a branch of the Earl of Home's, or Hume's; and my anceſtors had been proprietors of the eſtate, which my brother poſſeſſes, for ſeveral generations. My mother was daughter of Sir David

David Falconer, Prefident of the College of Juftice: the title of Lord Halkerton came by fucceffion to her brother.

My family, however, was not rich, and being myfelf a younger brother, my patrimony, according to the mode of my country, was of courfe very flender. My father, who paffed for a man of parts, died when I was an infant, leaving me, with an elder brother and a fifter, under the care of our mother, a woman of fingular merit, who, though young and handfome, devoted

her-

herſelf entirely to the rearing
and educating of her children.
I paſſed through the ordinary
courſe of education with ſucceſs,
and was ſeized very early with a
paſſion for literature, which has
been the ruling paſſion of my
life, and the great ſource of my
enjoyments. My ſtudious diſ-
poſition, my ſobriety, and my
induſtry, gave my family a notion that the law was a proper
profeſſion for me; but I found
an unſurmountable averſion to
every thing but the purſuits of
philoſophy and general learning;
and while they fancied I was
poring

poring upon Voet and Vinnius, Cicero and Virgil were the authors which I was secretly devouring.

My very slender fortune, however, being unsuitable to this plan of life, and my health being a little broken by my ardent application, I was tempted, or rather forced, to make a very feeble trial for entering into a more active scene of life. In 1734, I went to Bristol, with some recommendations to eminent merchants, but in a few months found that scene totally

unsuitunfuitable to me. I went over to France, with a view of profecuting my ftudies in a country retreat; and I there laid that plan of life, which I have fteadily and fuccefsfully purfued. I refolved to make a very rigid frugality fupply my deficiency of fortune, to maintain unimpaired my independency, and to regard every object as contemptible, except the improvement of my talents in literature.

During my retreat in France, firft at Reims, but chiefly at La Fleche, in Anjou, I compofed posed my *Treatise of Human Nature*. After passing three years very agreeably in that country, I came over to London in 1737. In the end of 1738, I published my Treatise, and immediately went down to my mother and my brother, who lived at his country-house, and was employing himself very judiciously and successfully in the improvement of his fortune.

Never literary attempt was more unfortunate than my Treatise of Human Nature. It fell

B 4 *dead-*

dead-born from the preſs, without reaching ſuch diſtinction, as
even to excite a murmur among
the zealots. But being naturally
of a cheerful and ſanguine temper, I very ſoon recovered the
blow, and proſecuted with great
ardour my ſtudies in the country. In 1742, I printed at Edinburgh the firſt part of my Eſſays:
the work was favourably received, and ſoon made me entirely
forget my former diſappoint-
ment. I continued with my
mother and brother in the country, and in that time recovered

the

the knowledge of the Greek language, which I had too much neglected in my early youth.

In 1745, I received a letter from the Marquis of Annandale, inviting me to come and live with him in England; I found alſo, that the friends and family of that young nobleman were deſirous of putting him under my care and direction, for the ſtate of his mind and health required it.—I lived with him a twelvemonth. My appointments during that time made a conſiderable acceſſion to my ſmall fortune.

tune. I then received an invitation from General St. Clair to attend him as a secretary to his expedition, which was at first meant against Canada, but ended in an incursion on the coast of France. Next year, to wit, 1747, I received an invitation from the General to attend him in the same station in his military embassy to the courts of Vienna and Turin. I then wore the uniform of an officer, and was introduced at these courts as aid-de-camp to the general, along with Sir Harry Erskine and Captain Grant, now Gene-

ral

ral Grant. Thefe two years were almoft the only interruptions which my ftudies have received during the courfe of my life: I paffed them agreeably, and in good company ; and my appointments, with my frugality, had made me reach a fortune, which I called independent, though moft of my friends were inclined to fmile when I faid fo; in fhort, I was now mafter of near a thoufand pounds.

I had always entertained a notion, that my want of fuccefs in publifhing the Treatife of Human

Human Nature, had proceeded more from the manner than the matter, and that I had been guilty of a very ufual indifcretion, in going to the prefs too early. I, therefore, caft the firft part of that work anew in the Enquiry concerning Human Underftanding, which was publifhed while I was at Turin. But this piece was at firft little more fuccefsful than the Treatife of Human Nature. On my return from Italy, I had the mortification to find all England in a ferment, on account of Dr. Middleton's Free Enquiry, while my performance was

was entirely overlooked and neglected. A new edition, which had been publifhed at London of my Effays, moral and political, met not with a much better reception.

Such is the force of natural temper, that thefe difappointments made little or no impreffion on me. I went down in 1749, and lived two years with my brother at his country-houfe, for my mother was now dead. I there compofed the fecond part of my Effays, which I called Political Difcourfes, and alfo my

‡ Enquiry

Enquiry concerning the Principles of Morals, which is another part of my treatife that I
caft anew. Meanwhile, my
bookfeller, A. Millar, informed
me, that my former publications
(all but the unfortunate Treatife)
were beginning to be the fubject
of converfation; that the fale
of them was gradually increaf-
ing, and that new editions were
demanded. Anfwers by Reverends, and Right Reverends,
came out two or three in a year;
and I found, by Dr. Warburton's
railing, that the books were beginning to be efteemed in good
com-

company. However, I had fix‐
ed a refolution, which I inflexi‐
bly maintained, never to reply
to any body ; and not being
very irafcible in my temper, I
have eafily kept myfelf clear of
all literary fquabbles. Thefe
fymptoms of a rifing reputation
gave me encouragement, as I
was ever more difpofed to fee the
favourable than unfavourable fide
of things ; a turn of mind which
it is more happy to poffefs, than
to be born to an eftate of ten
thoufand a year.

In

In 1751, I removed from the country to the town, the true scene for a man of letters. In 1752, were publifhed at Edinburgh, where I then lived, my Political Difcourfes, the only work of mine that was fuccefsful on the firft publication. It was well received abroad and at home. In the fame year was publifhed at London, my Enquiry concerning the Principles of Morals ; which, in my own opinion (who ought not to judge on that fubject), is of all my writings, hiftorical, philofophical, or literary, incomparably the beft. It

came

came unnoticed and unobferved into the world.

In 1752, the Faculty of Advocates chofe me their Librarian, an office from which I received little or no emolument, but which gave me the command of a large library. I then formed the plan of writing the Hiftory of England ; but being frightened with the notion of continuing a narrative through a period of 1700 years, I commenced with the acceffion of the Houfe of Stuart, an epoch when, I thought, the mifreprefentations of faction be-

C   gan

gan chiefly to take place. I was, I own, fanguine in my expecta- tions of the fuccefs of this work. I thought that I was the only hiftorian, that had at once ne- glected prefent power, intereft, and authority, and the cry of popular prejudices ; and as the fubject was fuited to every ca- pacity, I expected proportional applaufe. But miferable was my difappointment : I was affailed by one cry of reproach, difap- probation, and even deteftation ; Englifh, Scotch, and Irifh, Whig and Tory, churchman and fec- tary, freethinker and religionift,

patriot

patriot and courtier, united in their rage againſt the man, who had preſumed to ſhed a generous tear for the fate of Charles I. and the Earl of Strafford; and after the firſt ebullitions of their fury were over, what was ſtill more mortifying, the book ſeem-ed to ſink into oblivion. Mr. Millar told me, that in a twelve-month he ſold only forty-five copies of it. I ſcarcely, indeed, heard of one man in the three kingdoms, conſiderable for rank or letters, that could endure the book. I muſt only except the primate of England, Dr. Her-

C 2   ring,

ring, and the primate of Ireland, Dr. Stone, which feem two odd exceptions. Thefe dignified prelates feparately fent me meffages not to be difcouraged.

I was, however, I confefs, difcouraged ; and had not the war been at that time breaking out between France and England, I had certainly retired to fome provincial town of the former kingdom, have changed my name, and never more have returned to my native country. But as this fcheme was not now practicable, and the fubfequent volume was

con‹

confiderably advanced, I refolved to pick up courage and to per-
fevere.

In this interval, I publifhed
at London my Natural Hiftory
of Religion, along with fome
other fmall pieces: its public
entry was rather obfcure, except
only that Dr. Hurd wrote a
pamphlet againft it, with all the
illiberal petulance, arrogance,
and fcurrility, which diftinguifh
the Warburtonian fchool. This
pamphlet gave me fome con-
folation for the otherwife indiffe-
rent reception of my performance.

In 1756, two years after the
fall of the firſt volume, was
publiſhed the ſecond volume of
my Hiſtory, containing the period from the death of Charles I.
till the Revolution. This performance happened to give lefs
diſpleaſure to the Whigs, and
was better received. It not only
roſe itſelf, but helped to buoy up
its unfortunate brother.

But though I had been taught
by experience, that the Whig
party were in poſſeſſion of be-
ſtowing all places, both in the
ſtate and in literature, I was ſo
little

little inclined to yield to their fenfelefs clamour, that in above a hundred alterations, which farther ftudy, reading, or reflection engaged me to make in the reigns of the two firft Stuarts, I have made all of them invariably to the Tory fide. It is ridiculous to confider the Engfifh conftitution before that period as a regular plan of liberty.

In 1759, I publifhed my Hiftory of the Houfe of Tudor. The clamour againft this performance was almoft equal to that againft the Hiftory of the two

C 4 firft

firſt Stuarts. The reign of Elizabeth was particularly obnoxious. But I was now callous againſt the impreſſions of public folly, and continued very peaceably and contentedly in my retreat at Edinburgh, to finiſh, in two volumes, the more early part of the Engliſh Hiſtory, which I gave to the public in 1761, with tolerable, and but tolerable ſuccefs.

But, notwithſtanding this variety of winds and feaſons, to which my writings had been expoſed, they had ſtill been making

ing fuch advances, that the copy-
money given me by the book-
fellers, much exceeded any thing
formerly known in England; I
was become not only independent, but opulent. I retired to
my native country of Scotland,
determined never more to fet
my foot out of it; and retaining
the fatisfaction of never having
preferred a requeft to one great
man, or even making advances
of friendfhip to any of them. As
I was now turned of fifty, I
thought of paffing all the reft of
my life in this philofophical manner, when I received, in 1763,

an

an invitation from the Earl of
Hertford, with whom I was not
in the leaft acquainted, to attend
him on his embaffy to Paris, with
a near profpect of being appointed fecretary to the embaffy; and,
in the meanwhile, of performing
the functions of that office. This
offer, however inviting, I at firft
declined, both becaufe I was re-
luctant to begin connexions with
the great, and becaufe I was
afraid that the civilities and gay
company of Paris, would prove
difagreeable to a perfon of my
age and humour: but on his
lordfhip's repeating the invitation,

tion, I accepted of it. I have every reafon, both of pleafure and intereft, to think myfelf happy in my connexions with that nobleman, as well as af-terwards with his brother, General Conway.

Thofe who have not feen the ftrange effects of modes, will never imagine the reception I met with at Paris, from men and women of all ranks and ftations. The more I refiled from their exceffive civilities, the more I was loaded with them. There is, however, a real fatisfaction in

in living at Paris, from the
great number of fenfible, know-
ing, and polite company with
which that city abounds above
all places in the univerfe. I
thought once of fettling there
for life.

I was appointed fecretary to
the embaffy ; and, in fummer
1765, Lord Hertford left me,
being appointed Lord Lieutenant
of Ireland. I was *chargé d'af-*
faires till the arrival of the Duke
of Richmond, towards the end
of the year. In the beginning
of 1766, I left Paris, and next
fummer

fummer went to Edinburgh, with the fame view as formerly, of burying myfelf in a philofophical retreat. I returned to that place, not richer, but with much more money, and a much larger income, by means of Lord Hertford's friendfhip, than I left it; and I was defirous of trying what fuperfluity could produce, as I had formerly made an experiment of a competency. But, in 1767, I received from Mr. Conway an invitation to be Under-fecretary; and this invitation, both the character of the perfon, and my connexions with

8   Lord

Lord Hertford, prevented me from declining. I returned to Edinburgh in 1769, very opulent (for I poffeffed a revenue of 1000 l. a year), healthy, and though fomewhat ftricken in years, with the profpect of enjoying long my eafe, and of feeing the increafe of my reputation.

In fpring 1775, I was ftruck with a diforder in my bowels, which at firft gave me no alarm, but has fince, as I apprehend it, become mortal and incurable. I now reckon upon a fpeedy diffolution.

lution. I have fuffered very little pain from my diforder; and what is more ftrange, have, notwithftanding the great decline of my perfon, never fuffered a moment's abatement of my fpirits; infomuch, that were I to name the period of my life, which I fhould moft choofe to pafs over again, I might be tempted to point to this later period. I poffefs the fame ardour as ever in ftudy, and the fame gaiety in company. I confider, befides, that a man of fixty-five, by dying, cuts off only a few years of infirmities; and though I fee

*

many

many fymptoms of my literary
reputation's breaking out at laft
with additional luftre, I knew
that I could have but few years
to enjoy it. It is difficult to be
more detached from life than I
am at prefent.

To conclude hiftorically with
my own character. I am, or
rather was (for that is the ftyle
I muft now ufe in fpeaking of
myfelf, which emboldens me the
more to fpeak my fentiments); I
was, I fay, a man of mild dif-
pofitions, of command of temper, of an open, focial, and
cheerful

cheerful humour, capable of at-
tachment, but little fufceptible of
enmity, and of great moderation
in all my paffions. Even my
love of literary fame, my ruling
paffion, never foured my temper, notwithftanding my frequent
difappointments. My company
was not unacceptable to the
young and carelefs, as well as
to the ftudious and literary;
and as I took a particular pleafure in the company of modeft
women, I had no reafon to be
difpleafed with the reception I
met with from them. In a
word, though moft men any

D   wife

wife eminent, have found reafon to complain of calumny, I
never was touched, or even at-
tacked by her baleful tooth: and
though I wantonly expofed myfelf to the rage of both civil and
religious factions, they feemed
to be difarmed in my behalf of
their wonted fury. My friends
never had occafion to vindicate
any one circumftance of my character and conduct: not but that
the zealots, we may well fup-
pofe, would have been glad to
invent and propagate any ftory
to my difadvantage, but they
could never find any which they
thought

thought would wear the face of probability. I cannot fay there is no vanity in making this funeral oration of myfelf, but I hope it is not a mifplaced one; and this is a matter of fact which is eafily cleared and afcertained.

April 18, 1776.

D 2 LET-

LETTER

ADAM SMITH, LL.D.

TO

WILLIAM STRAHAN, Efq.

D 3

Kirkaldy, Fifeſhire, Nov. 9, 1776.

DEAR SIR,

IT is with a real, though a very melancholy pleaſure, that I ſit down to give you ſome account of the behaviour of our late excellent friend, Mr. Hume, during his laſt illneſs.

Though, in his own judgment, his diſeaſe was mortal and incurable, yet he allowed himſelf to be prevailed upon, by

D 4   the

the entreaty of his friends, to try what might be the effects of a long journey. A few days before he fet out, he wrote that account of his own life, which, together with his other papers, he has left to your care. My account, therefore, fhall begin where his ends.

He fet out for London towards the end of April, and at Morpeth met with Mr. John Home and myfelf, who had both come down from London on purpofe to fee him, expecting to have found him at Edinburgh.

Mr.

Mr. Home returned with him, and attended him during the whole of his ſtay in England, with that care and attention which might be expected from a temper ſo perfectly friendly and affectionate. As I had written to my mother that ſhe might expect me in Scotland, I was under the neceſſity of continuing my journey. His diſeaſe ſeemed to yield to exerciſe and change of air, and when he arrived in London, he was apparently in much better health than when he left Edinburgh. He was adviſed to go to Bath to drink the

waters,

waters, which appeared for some time to have so good an effect upon him, that even he himself began to entertain, what he was not apt to do, a better opinion of his own health. His symptoms, however, soon returned with their usual violence, and from that moment he gave up all thoughts of recovery, but submitted with the utmost cheerfulness, and the most perfect complacency and resignation. Upon his return to Edinburgh, though he found himself much weaker, yet his cheerfulness never abated, and he continued

to

to divert himfelf, as ufual, with
correcting his own works for a
new edition, with reading books
of amufement, with the converfation of his friends; and, fome-
times in the evening, with a
party at his favourite game of
whift. His cheerfulnefs was fo
great, and his converfation and
amufements run fo much in their
ufual ftrain, that, notwithftanding all bad fymptoms, many
people could not believe he was
dying. " I fhall tell your friend,
" Colonel Edmondftone," faid
Doctor Dundas to him one day,
" that I left you much better,

8 " and

" and in a fair way of recovery."
" Doctor," faid he, " as I be-
" lieve you would not chufe to
" tell any thing but the truth,
" you had better tell him, that
" I am dying as faft as my ene-
" mies, if I have any, could
" wifh, and as eafily and cheer-
" fully as my beft friends could
" defire." Colonel Edmondftone
foon afterwards came to fee him,
and take leave of him ; and on
his way home, he could not for-
bear writing him a letter bidding
him once more an eternal adieu,
and applying to him, as to a dying man, the beautiful French
verfes

verses in which the Abbé Chau-
lieu, in expectation of his own
death, laments his approaching
separation from his friend, the
Marquis de la Fare. Mr. Hume's
magnanimity and firmness were
such, that his most affectionate
friends knew, that they hazard-
ed nothing in talking or writing
to him as to a dying man, and
that so far from being hurt by
this frankness, he was rather
pleased and flattered by it. I
happened to come into his room
while he was reading this letter,
which he had just received, and
which he immediately showed

2   me.

me. I told him, that though I
was fenfible how very much he
was weakened, and that appear-
ances were in many refpects very
bad, yet his cheerfulnefs was ftill
fo great, the fpirit of life feemed ftill to be fo very ftrong in
him, that I could not help enter-
taining fome faint hopes. He an-
fwered, " Your hopes are ground-
" lefs.   An habitual diarrhœa of
" more than a year's ftanding,
" would be a very bad difeafe at
" any age : at my age it is a
" mortal one.   When I lie down
" in the evening, I feel myfelf
" weaker than when I rofe in the
                                    " morning ;

" morning; and when I rife in the
" morning, weaker than when I
" lay down in the evening. I am
" fenfible, befides, that fome of my
" vital parts are affected, fo that
" I muft foon die." " Well,"
faid I, " if it muft be fo, you
have at leaft the fatisfaction of
leaving all your friends, your
brother's family in particular,
in great profperity." He faid
that he felt that fatisfaction fo
fenfibly, that when he was reading a few days before, Lucian's
Dialogues of the Dead, among
all the excufes which are alleg-
ed to Charon for not entering
readily

readily into his boat, he could
not find one that fitted him ; he
had no houfe to finifh, he had
no daughter to provide for, he
had no enemies upon whom he
wifhed to revenge himfelf. " I
" could not well imagine," faid
he, " what excufe I could make to
" Charon in order to obtain a little
" delay. I have done every thing
" of confequence which I ever
" meant to do, and I could at no
" time expect to leave my relations
" and friends in a better fituation
" than that in which I am now
" likely to leave them ; I, there-
" fore, have all reafon to die con-
" tented."

" tented." He then diverted himfelf with inventing feveral jocu-
lar excufes, which he fuppofed
he might make to Charon, and
with imagining the very furly
anfwers which it might fuit the
character of Charon to return to
them. " Upon further con-
" fideration," faid he, " I
" thought I might fay to him,
" Good Charon, I have been
" correcting my works for a new
" edition. Allow me a little
" time, that I may fee how the
" Public receives the alterations."
But Charon would anfwer,
" When you have feen the effect
E " of

" of thefe, you will be for mak-
" ing other alterations. There
" will be no end of fuch excufes;
" fo, honeft friend, pleafe ftep
" into the boat." But I might
ftill urge, " Have a little pa-
" tience, good Charon, I have
" been endeavouring to open
" the eyes of the Public. If I
" live a few years longer, I may
" have the fatisfaction of feeing
" the downfal of fome of the
" prevailing fyftems of fuperfti-
" tion." But Charon would
then lofe all temper and decency.
" You loitering rogue, that will
" not happen thefe many hun-
" dred

" dred years. Do you fancy I
" will grant you a leafe for fo
" long a term ? Get into the
" boat this inftant, you lazy
" loitering rogue."

' But, though Mr. Hume always talked of his approaching
diffolution with great cheerfulnefs, he never affected to make
any parade of his magnanimity.
He never mentioned the fubject
but when the converfation naturally led to it, and never dwelt
longer upon it than the courfe
of the converfation happened to
require : it was a fubject indeed

E 2   which

which occurred pretty frequently,
in confequence of the inquiries
which his friends, who came to
fee him, naturally made concerning the ftate of his health. The
converfation which I mentioned
above, and which paffed on
Thurfday the 8th of Auguft,
was the laft, except one, that I
ever had with him. He had
now become fo very weak, that
the company of his moft intimate
friends fatigued him ; for his
cheerfulnefs was ftill fo great,
his complaifance and focial dif-
pofition were ftill fo entire, that
when any friend was with him,

he

he could not help talking more, and with greater exertion, than fuited the weaknefs of his body. At his own defire, therefore, I agreed to leave Edinburgh, where I was ftaying partly upon his account, and returned to my mother's houfe here, at Kirkaldy, upon condition that he would fend for me whenever he wifhed to fee me; the phyfician who faw him moft frequently, Doctor Black, undertaking, in the mean time, to write me occafionally an account of the ftate of his health.

On

On the 22d of Auguft, the Doctor wrote me the following letter :

" Since my laft, Mr. Hume has paffed his time pretty eafily, but is much weaker. He fits up, goes down ftairs once a day, and amufes himfelf with read-ing, but feldom fees any body. He finds that even the converfa-tion of his moft intimate friends fatigues and oppreffes him ; and it is happy that he does not need it, for he is quite free from anxiety, impatience, or low fpi-rits, and paffes his time very well

well with the affiftance of amuf-
ing books."

I received the day after a letter from Mr. Hume himfelf, of
which the following is an ex-
tract.

Edinburgh, 23d Auguft, 1776.

" MY DEAREST FRIEND,

" I am obliged to make ufe
of my nephew's hand in writing to you, as I do not rife to-
day.   *   *   *   *
*   *   *   *   *

E 4   " I go

" I go very faft to decline, and laft night had a fmall fever, which I hoped might put a quicker period to this tedious illnefs, but unluckily it has, in a great meafure, gone off. I cannot fubmit to your coming over here on my account, as it is poffible for me to fee you fo fmall a part of the day, but Doctor Black can better inform you concerning the degree of ftrength which may from time to time remain with me. A-dieu, &c."

Three

Three days after I received the following letter from Doctor Black.

Edinburgh, Monday, 26th August, 1776.

" DEAR SIR,

" Yesterday about four o'clock afternoon, Mr. Hume expired. The near approach of his death became evident in the night between Thursday and Friday, when his disease became excessive, and soon weakened him so much, that he could no longer rise out of his bed. He continued to the last perfectly sensible,

fible, and free from much pain
or feelings of diftrefs. He never
dropped the fmalleft expreffion
of impatience; but when he had
occafion to fpeak to the people
about him, always did it with
affection and tendernefs. I
thought it improper to write
to bring you over, efpecially as
I heard that he had dictated a
letter to you defiring you not to
come. When he became very
weak, it coft him an effort to
fpeak, and he died in fuch a
happy compofure of mind, that
nothing could exceed it."

＊　　　　　　　Thus

. Thus died our most excellent, and never to be forgotten friend ; concerning whose philosophical opinions men will, no doubt, judge varioufly, every one approving, or condemning them, according as they happen to coincide or difagree with his own; but concerning whose character and conduct there can scarce be a difference of opinion. His temper, indeed, feemed to be more happily balanced, if I may be allowed fuch an expreffion, than that perhaps of any other man I have ever known. Even in the loweft ftate of his
fortune,

fortune, his great and neceſſary frugality never hindered him from exerciſing, upon proper occaſions, acts both of charity and generoſity. It was a frugality founded, not upon avarice, but upon the love of independency. The extreme gentleneſs of his nature never weakened either the firmneſs of his mind, or the ſteadineſs of his reſolutions. His conſtant pleaſantry was the genuine effuſion of good-nature and good-humour, tempered with delicacy and modeſty, and without even the ſlighteſt tincture of maligni-
ty,

ty, fo frequently the difagreeable fource of what is called wit
in other men. It never was the
meaning of his raillery to mor-
tify; and therefore, far from
offending, it feldom failed to
pleafe and delight, even thofe
who were the objects of it. To
his friends, who were frequently the objects of it, there was not
perhaps any one of all his great
and amiable qualities, which
contributed more to endear his
converfation. And that gaiety
of temper, fo agreeable in fo-
ciety, but which is fo often ac-
companied with frivolous and
fuper-

ſuperficial qualities, was in him certainly attended with the moſt ſevere application, the moſt extenſive learning, the greateſt depth of thought, and a capacity in every reſpect the moſt comprehenſive. Upon the whole, I have always conſidered him, both in his lifetime and ſince his death, as approaching as nearly to the idea of a perfectly wiſe and virtuous man, as perhaps the nature of human frailty will permit,

I ever am, dear Sir,

Moſt affectionately your's,

ADAM SMITH,